# 20,000 Leagues Under the Sea

ADAPTED BY: Jan Fields
ILLUSTRATED BY: Eric Scott Fisher

magic
wagon

**visit us at www.abdopublishing.com**

Published by Magic Wagon, a division of the ABDO Group,
8000 West 78th Street, Edina, Minnesota 55439. Copyright
© 2011 by Abdo Consulting Group, Inc. International copyrights
reserved in all countries. All rights reserved. No part of this
book may be reproduced in any form without written permission
from the publisher.

Calico Chapter Books™ is a trademark and logo of Magic Wagon.

Printed in the United States of America, Melrose Park, Illinois.
102010
012011

 This book contains at least 10% recycled materials.

Original text by Jules Verne
Adapted by Jan Fields
Illustrated by Eric Scott Fisher
Edited by Stephanie Hedlund and Rochelle Baltzer
Cover and interior design by Abbey Fitzgerald

**Library of Congress Cataloging-in-Publication Data**

Fields, Jan.
  20,000 leagues under the sea / Jules Verne ; adapted by Jan Fields ;
illustrated by Eric Scott Fisher.
    p. cm. -- (Calico illustrated classics)
  ISBN 978-1-61641-110-7
  [1. Sea stories. 2. Submarines (Ships)--Fiction. 3. Science fiction.]  I.
Fisher, Eric Scott, ill. II. Verne, Jules, 1828-1905. Vingt mille lieues
sous les mers. III. Title. IV. Title: Twenty thousand leagues under the
sea.
  PZ7.F479177Aap 2010
  [Fic]--dc22
                                        2010030857

# Table of Contents

# CHAPTER 1

# A Shifting Reef

The year 1866 was marked by strange events at sea. Several ships met with a long, glowing object of enormous size. The thing moved incredibly fast and had no set migration or patch of ocean in which to dwell.

It might have been allowed to exist in peace had it not done the one unforgivable thing—it endangered ships. And specifically it damaged a ship owned by the famous English shipowner Cunard.

In April 1867, the *Scotia* was struck by something that pierced its hull with a neat hole in the shape of a perfect triangle. The ship limped home safely, but the damage was enough to bring about the public outcry to rid the seas of this mysterious creature.

At this time, I was in the United States. The French government had asked me to join an expedition to the Badlands of Nebraska. This was because I was an assistant professor at the Museum of Natural History in Paris. By the end of March, I was in New York packing for my return to Paris.

I was familiar with the stories of the mysterious sea creature. They filled every newspaper. Some said the creature was really floating debris from a wreck or a floating reef. But that hardly explained the high speeds some witnessed.

Some said it was some kind of underwater boat, but how could any country create such an amazing craft in complete secrecy? And to what purpose?

Each country was questioned, of course. But every government seemed equally concerned about this dangerous situation.

During my stay in New York, several people consulted me on the subject. Finally, I did share my opinion with the *New York Herald*. I considered each theory and responded to it.

Finally, I admitted that I believed the creature was a giant narwhal. The narwhal can grow to sixty feet and has a long tusk that has been known to pierce the sides of wooden ships. I believed we were seeing a species ten times the normal size.

My theory was hotly debated, but I heard no better ideas presented. I admit my theory added fuel to the "monster hunters." They insisted the creature be tracked down and eliminated.

The United States planned a mission to hunt the narwhal. The fast frigate, the *Abraham Lincoln*, was called to fulfill the mission with Commander Farragut in charge.

Three hours before the *Abraham Lincoln* was due to leave its pier in Brooklyn, I received the following letter:

*Pierre Aronnax*
*Professor of the Paris Museum*
*Fifth Avenue Hotel, New York*

*Dear Sir,*
*If you would like to join the expedition of the* Abraham Lincoln, *the government of the United States would take great pleasure in having you represent France on this mission.*
*Cordially yours,*
*J.B. Hobson*
*Secretary of the Navy*

Though I had given no thought to chasing the narwhal, I decided at once that I must go. I called my servant and assistant, Conseil, and told him we had two hours to prepare and reach the ship. He agreed with complete calm, only asking what to do with my many collections.

"The hotel will keep them for us," I assured him.

"Whatever suits Monsieur," he said.

We arrived at the *Abraham Lincoln* as it was preparing to leave. Commander Farragut welcomed me in person and I was quickly taken to my cabin, which I found pleasant. We then left port as crowds cheered from the wharves lining the East River.

# CHAPTER 2

# At Full Speed

Commander Farragut had sworn to get rid of the giant narwhal, and no other course was acceptable. He promised $2,000 to the first man to spot the whale. This guaranteed the enthusiasm of virtually every man aboard.

The ship was outfitted with hand-thrown harpoons, blunderbusses that shot out barbed arrows, and swivel guns with exploding shells. On the forecastle stood a cannon.

With all this weaponry onboard, the ship had something even better—the best harpooner in the world. Ned Land had skill, courage, and coolness. No whale was likely to escape him.

Land was a tall, powerfully built Canadian. He could be hot tempered, but he took a special liking to me, as he enjoyed conversing in French. He also did not believe in the giant narwhal.

"I've hunted hundreds of whales," he said. "But none could crack the steel plates of a steamer, not with tails nor tusks."

"But we know narwhals have pierced the sides of ships," I argued.

"Wooden ships," the Canadian said.

"But if the whale doesn't exist," I said. "How do you explain what happened to the *Scotia?*"

Land had no answer but still doubted the giant narwhal's existence. I believed he would soon find reason to change his mind.

For months, the *Abraham Lincoln* cruised down the Atlantic coast of South America and on to the Pacific. We found nothing but water.

Finally, the crew's enthusiasm waned. No one spoke of mutiny, of course. Still, Commander Farragut felt the crew's mood.

On November 2, he promised to look just three more days. If nothing was spotted, we would head for European waters and then home.

The three days passed and Commander Farragut changed course. On that night, I stood at the rail and looked across the water. Conseil stood at my side, as he always did.

"This was a foolish venture," I said sadly. "I expect people will laugh at my theory now."

"Yes," Conseil answered calmly. "People will laugh at Monsieur, and Monsieur will be getting what he deserves."

"Really?"

"An honored scientist like Monsieur does not get mixed up in . . ."

But Conseil did not get the chance to finish scolding me, for Land's voice rang out. "Ahoy! There it is!"

And so it was at a distance of about 400 yards off the starboard quarter. There could be no mistake about it. The creature was several fathoms below the surface, giving off a huge oval-shaped glow.

Then the creature began moving toward us. The frigate moved rapidly away. Or rather, it tried to move away, but the creature moved at double the speed of the ship. The creature did a complete circle around us, then moved off about two or three miles.

Suddenly, it rushed headlong toward the *Abraham Lincoln* at a terrifying speed. It dove beneath us and came up on the other side.

"Get up more speed if you can," Land suggested. "I'll take up position in the bowsprit. If we can get near enough, I'll harpoon it."

The commander called out, "Build up more pressure."

The *Abraham Lincoln* reached an unheard of speed of 18.5 knots, but the creature simply traveled at the same rate and allowed not one inch of gain.

More coal was shoveled into the boilers. Our speed reached 19.3 knots. We were in real danger of blowing up, but we still could not catch the creature.

Finally the commander called for the best gunner to man the forward cannon. The shell reached its target but only glanced off. Then the creature glided slowly toward us.

I leaned over the forward rail and could see Land below me. He was hanging on to the rigging and clutching his terrible harpoon.

When scarcely twenty feet remained between him and the creature, he threw the harpoon. I heard a ringing noise as the harpoon struck something hard. Then the light went out and two enormous streams of water broke over the deck of the frigate. It rushed from stem to stern.

There was a terrible crash. I was hurled overboard and into the sea.

# Ned Land's Tempers

At first, I was dragged down to a depth of about twenty feet. I am a good swimmer and I did not panic. Two strong kicks brought me back to the surface.

My first thought was the frigate. Did I have any chance of being saved? In the darkness, I could make out the vague black shape of the ship slowly fading as it got farther away. I was done for.

My wet clothes weighed down my body. I was sinking. I shouted for help and my mouth filled with water. Suddenly a powerful hand grabbed me, and I was pulled to the surface.

"If Monsieur would lean on my shoulder, Monsieur would be able to swim more comfortably."

I seized the arm of my faithful Conseil. "Did the crash throw you into the water along with me?" I asked.

"Not at all. I followed Monsieur."

"And the frigate?" I asked.

Conseil rolled over on his back. "I think Monsieur would be wise not to count on that too much. When I was getting ready to jump into the water, I heard men shouting that the propeller and rudder were broken."

"That means we're done for!"

"Nevertheless, we still have several hours," Conseil answered calmly. "And one can do many things in several hours."

Conseil's unshakable coolness gave me courage. Conseil used a knife he carried to cut my clothes from me, and then I did the same for him. We could swim more comfortably now.

We decided to take turns swimming in the direction of the frigate. One man would relax completely while the other towed him and swam. We swam this way for several hours.

Finally, the moon appeared over the edge of a large cloud and we were able to see more clearly. I caught sight of the frigate. It was over five miles away. I was too exhausted to make a sound, but Conseil shouted for help.

It seemed as if I heard someone answer his shout. Conseil shouted again and this time there could be no doubt about it. A human voice was answering ours.

Conseil pushed me along until something hard knocked against me. I grabbed onto it. I felt something dragging me, and I passed out.

I opened my eyes to the fading light of the moon sinking down toward the horizon. I made out a face that wasn't Conseil's but that I immediately recognized.

"Ned!" I cried.

"Yes, it's me, still chasing my prize," the Canadian answered.

"Were you thrown into the sea by the collision?" I asked.

"Yes," he said. "But I was able to catch a ride on our monster. I can see now why my harpoon couldn't do any damage. This critter is covered in steel plates."

In shock, I felt beneath me and my hand rested on bolted down plates. This monster was the work of man.

"This thing must have some form of crew," I said.

"Obviously," replied the harpooner. "But I've been on this thing for three hours and have seen no sign of life."

"It hasn't moved?"

"We know it's capable of great speed. It must have a crew." Just then, there was a swirling in the water to the rear of the strange thing and it began moving. We got a good hold of its top side and rode along.

"As long as it stays on the surface," Land murmured. "We should be all right."

We knew the ship could dive. So it was urgent that we communicate with its crew. I tried to find some opening or hatch, but found only smooth plate.

Toward four in the morning, the ship picked up speed. It became difficult to hang on. Luckily, Land found a large mooring ring and we were able to get a firm hold on it.

Finally dawn came. With it, the ship began to sink slowly. Ned Land pounded the steel plates with the heel of his boot.

"Confound it," he shouted. "Open up!"

A loud clanking rang from inside the submarine. One of the plates rose up and a man appeared. He cried out and quickly disappeared. Then eight young men with masked faces came out on deck and dragged us inside.

# CHAPTER 4

# Some Figures

When the hatch closed behind us, I was surrounded by total darkness. I could feel a ladder under my feet. At the bottom of the ladder, we were hauled into a room. A steel door slammed, closing us into the total darkness.

Land raged around the room in a fury. "Calm down, Ned," Conseil urged. "We must think calmly."

"Well, I've still got my bowie knife and I know how to use it," Land shouted.

As they spoke, I felt around in the dark. The bare walls were without doors or windows and a thick linen mat covered the floor. I walked into a wooden table surrounded by stools but found nothing else.

About half an hour after being tossed into the room, a blinding light came on from an electric bulb in the ceiling.

"Finally!" said Land, who stood with his knife in hand. "We can see."

"But we are still in the dark," I muttered. The light allowed me to see the small room but showed nothing interesting. From within it, I could not even tell if the submarine was moving. Still, the sudden light suggested to me that we might soon be visited.

We heard bolts drawn and the door opened to show two men. One of the men was short but powerfully built with broad shoulders and a large head. He wore a big mustache.

The other man had pale skin and a calm confidence. He was tall with splendid teeth and piercing, wide-set eyes. Both men wore otter-skin caps and seal-skin boots. The tall man looked each of us over and then spoke in some deep language that I didn't recognize.

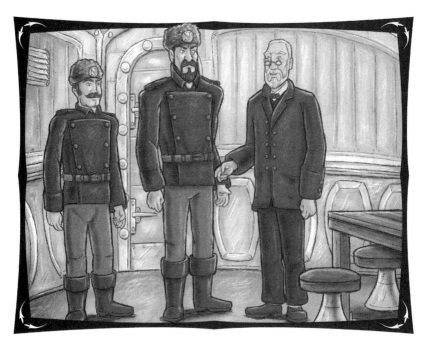

The other man nodded in response and answered in equally incomprehensible words. Then the shorter man looked at me. I told him in French that I did not speak his language. He looked puzzled.

"Monsieur should tell them our story anyway," Conseil whispered. "They may understand some words."

And so I did, speaking carefully and not omitting a single detail. I then formally presented each of us by name.

Neither of the men spoke in response so I asked Land to tell them our story in English. Land's telling of our tale was basically the same as mine but more emotional and colorful. He ended his tale by mentioning that we were dying of hunger.

Again, the men showed no sign of understanding. "If you wish," Conseil said, "I could try German."

I looked at him in surprise. "You speak German?"

"No better than most Belgians," he said.

I told him to try and he did. German received no more reaction than French or English. So I tried Latin. I expect my pronunciation was horrible, but I muddled through.

The men then looked at one another, exchanged a few words and shut us into the room again.

"I believe they made up their own private language just to annoy decent people who want a bite of supper," Land grumbled.

Just as he spoke, the door opened and a steward came in. He brought us fresh clothing, and we dressed quickly as the man set the table for three. Though we were given only water to drink, the food was delicious.

I noticed that each utensil was embossed with an "N" surrounded by a circle and the words *Mobilis in Mobile*.

After we each had a full stomach, Land and Conseil stretched out on the floor and soon fell asleep. I sat down and pondered the mysteries set before me for some time before sleep crept over me as well.

# CHAPTER
## 5

# The Man of the Seas

I awoke before my companions and saw the steward had cleared the table while we slept. As I waited for my friends to waken, I noticed an odd weight in my chest. The air felt heavy and I was soon panting slightly for breath.

I wondered how this huge submarine renewed its air supply and hoped whatever method it used would happen soon. Suddenly, I felt a current of pure air with a strong smell of salt.

I opened my mouth wide and allowed my lungs to soak up the air. I could also feel a slight rolling movement and I assumed the submarine has surfaced to take on fresh air.

Land and Conseil woke then.

"I smell sea air," Land said. I told them what had happened while they slept. He looked around the room and grumbled that even without a clock he knew it was mealtime. I felt hungry as well, but could see no way to get food any sooner than our hosts should choose to provide it.

Land's temper grew shorter as he grew hungrier. He ranted about being a prisoner. He shouted and yelled. He banged on the walls. I began to wonder myself if our fate had been decided and it was not a pleasant one.

Just then, we heard a noise and the door opened. Before I could do anything, the Canadian launched himself at the poor steward and began choking him. Conseil and I pulled at the burly harpooner's hands.

Suddenly, a voice spoke in French, "Calm down, Master Land." It was the tall captain of the ship. At these words, Land released the steward, who left after a word from the captain.

"You speak French," I said foolishly.

"As well as English, German, and Latin. I understood your story each time it was spoken. I merely needed time to decide what to do about your coming to disturb my life."

"Involuntarily," I said.

"Oh?" The captain looked at me sharply. "So the *Abraham Lincoln* wasn't looking for this vessel? It didn't fire upon me?"

"We believed this ship to be a creature that endangered ships," I said.

A half smile played about his lips. "Monsieur Aronnax, would you have me believe that the frigate would not have fired upon me if it had known this was a submarine?"

I knew that Commander Farragut would have, so I remained silent.

"So you have come to me as enemies," the captain said. "And I would be perfectly at rights to put you outside and dive."

"Surely, that would not be the choice of a civilized man," I cried.

The captain's face grew white with fury.

"Professor, do not ever refer to me as a civilized man again," he said. "I want no contact with civilized men."

The room was perfectly silent for a long moment. Then the captain spoke more quietly. "Since fate has put you here, you will remain onboard. You will be free to move about as you like unless you are called upon to remain in your cabins. If you can accept such an order on the rare occasion that I must give it, I will give you complete liberty aboard this ship."

"We accept," I said.

"But one thing is certain," Land said. "I will never give my word not to try to escape!"

"I do not need your word on that score," the captain said. "But I will live out the rest of my life on this vessel and so shall all of you."

We took a moment to absorb his words and then he spoke again. "As a man of science, Professor, I believe you will find much here to interest you. You are well-respected in your field, but you know only what the earth can tell you. Here you will learn the secrets of a totally different world."

I cannot deny that I felt a thrill at those words. "So, Captain, can you tell me what we should call you and what we should call this amazing craft?" I asked.

"For you, I shall be merely Captain Nemo," he said. "And you all will be my passengers on the *Nautilus*. And now it is time for lunch."

A fresh steward appeared and led Land and Conseil away to their cabin for a meal. The captain invited me to join him for his lunch and I followed him.

We went down a short, electrically lit corridor, then entered another room about thirty feet away. The dining room held two high oak sideboards inlaid with ebony. On their shelves lay china, porcelain, and a silver dinner service. In the center of the room was a richly set table.

"Sit," the captain said as he gestured toward a chair. "You must be hungry. I assure you this food is safe and healthy."

"Is this all from the sea?" I asked.

"Yes, the sea furnishes me with everything I need. I never eat the flesh of land animals. What looks like steak," he said, "is turtle. Dolphin liver is much like stewed pork. Our cream is from whale's milk and our anemone jam is as good as that made from the most delicious fruit."

I tasted everything and found it delicious. "You love the sea, don't you, Captain?"

"Yes, I do," he replied. "It nourishes me. It also clothes me in cloth made from the filaments of certain shellfish. I write with a pen of whalebone and use ink from cuttlefish. Everything comes from the sea and someday I will return to it."

Then as I set my napkin aside, my stomach full, the captain said, "And now if you would like a tour of the *Nautilus*, I am at your disposal."

# CHAPTER 6

# All by Electricity

I followed the captain through a double door at the back of the dining room. The next room was set up as a library. High bookcases of black Brazilian rosewood lined the walls. Nearby were leather couches.

Small wooden desks could be pulled up to the couches for working. In the middle of the room, a large table held pamphlets and old newspapers.

"You have a huge collection," I said, looking around the room.

"Twelve thousand books. I bought my last book and papers on the day I left land and I like to think that nothing of consequence has been written since. Please, feel free to use this space whenever you like."

I looked over the books and found them mostly relating to science and practical matters of engineering. There was nothing relating to politics or philosophy, though he had a substantial section of fiction and poetry.

I checked the dates on the newspapers. The *Nautilus* must have launched in 1865, three years before.

"Thank you," I said to Nemo. "I know I will enjoy many hours of study here."

Then Nemo opened another door and I was led into a huge, splendidly lit lounge. It was a veritable museum, filled with treasures of art and nature.

I saw masterworks by the greatest artists of all time and I stared like a child. I wandered through the room and spotted a large organ against one of the walls, musical scores by Mozart, Beethoven, and Haydn showed Nemo's taste in music was as classical as his taste in art.

Next to these works of art were rarities of nature. They consisted mainly of plants, shells, and other products of the sea but in amazing variety.

The room also held a large fountain made from a single clam shell. The collection of shells and corals was beyond anything I had seen in any museum in the world. The array of colors and sizes of pearls alone would be worth a king's riches. It was impossible to estimate the value of the total collection.

Then Nemo asked me to follow him again and he showed me my cabin. It was an elegant room to match the best hotels. Then he took me to the captain's cabin. It was equally large but furnished only with necessities, as if the captain needed no comforts.

Nemo asked me to sit. Then he showed me a variety of devices he used to navigate the *Nautilus*.

I recognized many of the tools, such as a thermometer, a compass, and a sextant. He also had devices unique to an underwater craft, such as pressure gauges.

"The *Nautilus* is driven by electricity," Captain Nemo said. "Electricity allows me to do what cannot be done by wind in sails or steam in engines."

"The results you get from electricity are quite amazing."

"I use it for some of my instruments as well," Nemo said, pointing to a dial. "This dial calculates the speed of the *Nautilus* and tells me we are cruising right now at fifteen knots. You can also find these same gauges in the lounge, all connected by electricity to provide the information I need wherever I am."

"Marvelous," I said.

"We're not through with our tour," the captain said as he got up. "Let us visit the aft of the *Nautilus*."

I saw that each door and section had watertight bulkheads that could be sealed with rubber gaskets around the edge. Thus if a leak began in one part of the submarine, it could be quickly sealed off.

Nemo pointed to an iron ladder in a kind of well between two bulkheads. He told me it led to a small boat they sometimes used to go fishing or just to be out under the sky for a bit.

"When I am finished with my little outing, the *Nautilus* comes to me," Captain Nemo said. "I remain attached to it by an electric wire and I send them a message."

He showed me more electric wonders as we proceeded. In the kitchen, all the cooking was done by electricity passing through platinum sponges to give off an even heat. Electricity was also used to heat a vast tank of water, which then evaporated and condensed to make the freshwater aboard ship.

Finally, he brought me to the engine room. There, the strange battery-powered engines drove the ship at speeds up to fifty knots. I was quite overwhelmed by all that I saw, but he wasn't done revealing the wonders of the *Nautilus*.

Nemo led me back to the comfortable seats of the library. Once seated, he explained the diving abilities of the ship.

"The *Nautilus* has two hulls, one inside the other to give it the strength needed to dive deeply," Nemo explained. "We take on water in our ballast to sink and pump it out to rise. And the dynamic power of the *Nautilus*'s engines is nearly infinite!"

"But how can you steer a course inside this solid ship?" I asked.

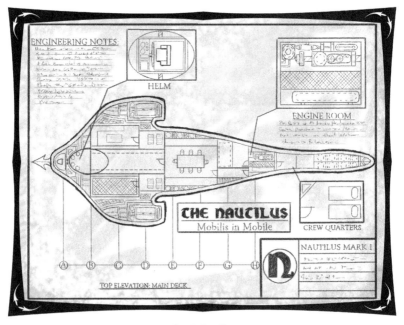

"The helmsman is inside a special compartment on the top of the hull that is equipped with windows."

"You have glass that can stand up under such pressures?"

"Absolutely. The lenses I use are more than eight inches thick at their centers. Also, behind the helmsman's compartment there is a powerful electric light that's rays illuminate the water for half a mile around."

"Bravo," I said with a laugh. "That explains the glow. But why did you strike the *Scotia*?"

"Completely accidental and the damage was not serious."

"Well, I certainly see that the *Nautilus* is an extraordinary ship," I said.

"Yes," Nemo said with real emotion. "I love it as if it were my own flesh and blood!"

"How could you construct such a wonder without anyone knowing?"

"I designed it in sections and had bits of it made all over the world. Then I built a workshop on a private island where we put the pieces together. After we launched, every trace was destroyed in a fire on the deserted island."

"You must be very rich to undertake such an expense."

"With building and furnishing, it cost close to a million dollars," he said. "And I am rich. I could easily pay France's entire national debt."

At that, I could merely stare in wonder.

# CHAPTER 7

# A Note of Invitation

"Professor, if you would like to join me," Nemo said. "I am going to take our bearings and determine our point of departure for the voyage."

The captain pressed a button three times and the pumps began to expel the water that held us beneath the surface. The pressure gauge showed the *Nautilus* was rising.

I walked to the companionway leading up to the platform and climbed the iron steps. The platform was only a few feet above water level. I studied the iron plates of the *Nautilus* and saw they overlapped slightly like scales, giving it even more the appearance of a sea creature.

Toward the middle of the platform, the small detachable boat protruded slightly. I looked out across the sea and saw endless nothing. No reef, no island, no *Abraham Lincoln*. The captain measured the height of the sun with his sextant, thus getting his latitude.

As he finished up his readings, I took one last look at the sea, slightly yellow as it always was in these Pacific waters near Japan. When I followed Nemo back into the craft and down to his vast personal museum, he nodded toward me and said, "Now I leave you to your studies."

Alone in the lounge, I traced an idle finger over the maps and charts laid out on a table before me. Land and Conseil appeared at the door, gaping at the luxurious room.

"This is like the museum in Quebec," Land murmured.

"More like the Sommerand Palace," Conseil said.

"And yet we are in neither Canada nor France," I said, "but aboard the *Nautilus*, 165 feet below the surface of the Pacific Ocean."

"This astonishes even a Belgian like myself," Conseil said.

"Look around," I said. "For a good classifier like you, there are enough items to keep you busy for a good while."

Conseil soon stood peering into cases, mumbling the classes, families, and species found inside them. Land paid no attention to the cases but sat to quiz me on Nemo. I told him all I knew and asked what he had learned.

"Nothing," he grumbled. "I haven't even seen any of the crew. How many men are aboard? Ten, twenty, fifty, a hundred?"

I had no way to know, but I encouraged him to enjoy what he could see. The *Nautilus* was truly a marvel. Land shook his head and insisted the only thing to know about a prison was how to escape.

Suddenly the lights in the room went out, and we heard an odd sliding sound. Light entered from each side of the room. The walls had drawn back to expose glass panels that looked out at the water. We clustered near the closest window, peering through the glass like aquarium visitors.

"Unbelievable," Ned said. "Conseil, tell me the names of these fish!"

"I can't," Conseil said. "That's my master's job."

Although Conseil was an enthusiast classifier, he was not good at recognizing creatures without a label.

"A triggerfish," I said, pointing.

"Genus, Balistes," Conseil said then. "Family of Sclerodermi and order of Plectognathi."

I also saw a Chinese ray, a green wrasse, a red mullet, and a violet spotted goby. The creatures passed us like a living rainbow. We kept up an constant commentary as the creatures passed.

Land could name many of the fish and Conseil would then classify them. The lounge lights came on again and the iron panels closed. Then, we returned to our cabins.

For the next several days, I saw no sign of Captain Nemo or any other crew member. Conseil and Land joined me for part of every day in the big lounge.

I began a diary to remember the wonders we saw and to help keep track of days. Each day when we surfaced to collect fresh air, I went out on the platform. I liked to enjoy the beauty of the sunrise and to spend time with no ceiling above me but the sky.

Finally, on November 16, I entered my cabin to find a note lying on my table. It was an invitation from Captain Nemo to go hunting with him the following morning. The note also invited Land and Conseil to join us.

"A hunting expedition!" Land cried. "And see it mentions the forests of Crespo Island so he must sometimes go ashore."

"It would seem so," I said. We looked up Crespo Island on the maps and found it about 1,800 miles from the point we had joined the

*Nautilus*. The island was tiny, but I still looked forward to the opportunity to leave the ship.

Nemo met us early the next morning in the big lounge. I asked him why we were having an excursion on an island, considering his feelings about dry land.

"The forests we shall visit are not on land, but underwater," he said.

"Then how can we explore them?" I asked.

"We will take our oxygen with us," he said. "I will show you, but eat hearty as there will not be another meal until evening. We can carry air on our hunt but not food."

"But the air you can take with you must get used up quickly," I said. "And then it's not fit for breathing."

"The *Nautilus*'s pumps allow me to store air under considerable pressure," Nemo responded. "I can store enough air to last nine or ten hours."

"And what do we do for light and guns?" I asked.

"You'll carry a bright light that runs on a Bunsen battery," Nemo explained. "And the gun uses air pressure to fire little glass capsules invented by the Austrian chemist Lenniebroek. They are little Leyden jars and when they break, an electrical charge enters the creature that knocks it quite dead."

With that, I had no other questions. After our meal, we followed Captain Nemo to the stern of the *Nautilus*. We entered a small room where we would put on our hunting costumes.

When Land saw the diving outfits, he decided not to go with us. "I'll never get into clothes like that unless they force me to."

"No one will force you, Ned," Nemo said.

"Is Conseil going to try it?" Land asked.

"I follow Monsieur wherever he goes," my loyal friend answered.

Two men from the crew helped us into the heavy, waterproof suits. They were made of rubber and felt like strong and supple armor.

The trousers ended in thick shoes with lead soles. The jacket used copper plates to protect the chest against water pressure and the sleeves ended in gloves.

A member of the crew handed me a rather ordinary-looking rifle that used compressed air for firing.

"How will we get to the ocean floor?" I asked as I examined the weapon.

"Right now the *Nautilus* is sitting on the bottom at a depth of thirty feet. We will merely walk out."

Then Captain Nemo put on his spherical helmet and Conseil and I did the same. The top part of our jackets ended in a threaded copper collar and the helmet attached to that.

Once fully dressed, I felt imprisoned in my clothes. They were so heavy that I could not make even a single step.

The crewmen helped us into a little compartment next to the dressing room. They sealed the door and I heard a whistling sound. Something cold rose from my feet to my chest and I knew the room was being flooded.

As soon as it filled, a second door in the hull of the *Nautilus* was opened and we stepped out on the ocean floor.

# CHAPTER 8

# A Walk

Captain Nemo and the crewman he had brought along led our group. Conseil and I followed, staying close to one another. My clothes no longer felt heavy.

We walked over fine-grained sand for hours, yet I felt little fatigue and no hunger at all. I admired the kaleidoscope of sea life we passed. Whenever I paused to admire something, Nemo would wave me on to keep going.

Finally Nemo stopped and pointed to several dark masses a short way off. The forest of Crespo was composed of large, treelike plants. Everything grew straight up toward the surface, changing shape only as I pushed them aside when I walked.

When we finally stopped to rest, I dozed off and awoke to find a huge spider crab eyeing me. I shuddered with horror as I rose to my feet, and Nemo's companion bashed the crab with his rifle butt. The crab writhed in horrible convulsions from the blow.

We walked on until we reached the very edge of the island. Nemo turned us around. The route back to the ship was steep and difficult.

Suddenly, the captain froze and shouldered his gun. It fired with a hissing sound and a sea otter fell dead several feet away. Nemo's companion threw the animal over his shoulder and we walked on.

Soon after, Nemo's companion shouldered his rifle and fired toward the surface. His shot struck a huge albatross, which was added to the crewman's burden.

As we walked on, I saw the vague glimmer of the *Nautilus*'s light and I was glad for it. The air I breathed had begun to grow heavy. Suddenly

Nemo turned and ran back toward me. He pushed me down into a shrub of seaweed as his companion did the same to Conseil.

From that position on my back, I saw huge sharks swirl past. I could clearly see their silver bellies and huge mouths bristling with teeth. But the sharks passed by us without notice.

A half an hour later we reached the *Nautilus*. I was exhausted, hungry, and happy to return to breathing the clear air of the submarine.

The next morning was November 18. I awakened refreshed and recovered from the previous day. As was my habit, I went up to the platform as the first mate did his morning gazing upon the ocean with his glass.

The ocean was deserted, as it had been since the beginning of our voyage. I looked over the waters and was surprised to see Captain Nemo come up. He did not acknowledge my presence but went about his calculations.

Then a good twenty sailors came on the platform to haul in the nets from their dragging of the sea. The nets held a huge collection of fish, and I looked them over quizzically as they were lowered through a hatch.

"Look at the ocean, Professor," the captain said, surprising me. "It is awakening after a peaceful night. It lives and breathes with the tides and with evaporation. It has a circulation of currents. It is a more intense life than you can find anywhere on dry land."

I didn't answer, as he seemed to be half speaking to himself. Finally we returned to the lounge and I heard the propeller start up.

Land and Conseil soon joined me. Conseil filled Land's ears with the story of our undersea adventure. Land vowed to join us if we were invited on another hunt.

Almost every day, the panels of the lounge remained open for several hours. We never grew tired of watching the show.

The *Nautilus* continued on a southeasterly course and each day slipped into another. In early December, we encountered an immense school of squid. They surely numbered in the millions as they migrated in the wake of herrings and sardines. I found the spectacle fascinating.

Not many days after, we saw something even more astonishing through the viewports. It was a ship with its severed shrouds still hanging. Its hull seemed to be in good condition and I suspect it had sunk only hours before.

On the deck, the body of a woman rose half out of a hatch on the poop deck, holding a child in her arms. Four sailors were frozen in the task of untwisting themselves from rigging ropes. The helmsman still clutched the wheel as if steering the ship through the ocean depths.

We were left speechless at the sight.

# A Few Days on Land

Soon, the *Nautilus* touched the Tropic of Capricorn and proceeded in a west by northwest direction. Above us, I knew the sun beat down without mercy, but we felt no effects as the ship slipped through coral islands.

Conseil asked me how long the tiny corals had been at work to build such huge reefs and islands.

"Scientists believe these coral reefs and islands grow a quarter inch per century," I said.

Conseil stared out at the massive walls of coral through the viewing ports. "Then we are seeing over a 100,000 years."

We passed more shipwrecks, most far older than the first we had seen.

"What a fine death for a sailor," Nemo said. "How tranquil is a coral tomb. May the heavens grant that my companions and I be buried in no other!"

On New Year's Day, I stood on the platform for my morning look across the sea. I knew we were not far from New Guinea. Conseil appeared on the platform and wished me a happy new year.

"Is it good?" I asked.

"I have had no time to be bored," Conseil said. "I have seen so many strange things. I look forward to what I may see in this new year."

"And how does Land feel?" I asked.

"He is not a man of science. He grows tired of seeing and not doing. And of eating fish."

Not many days after this, we were creeping through the Torres Strait between Australia and New Guinea. The sea boiled furiously where the waves dashed against hidden coral.

"What an awful stretch of water," Land said.

I agreed. Then as we passed within two miles of an island, the ship struck a reef with such violence that I was knocked off my feet.

My companions and I hurried up on the platform and spotted the captain. He looked as calm as ever.

"The *Nautilus* has run aground," I said.

"It is only a delay," he said. "In five days, the full moon will raise the tide high enough to lift us from this reef."

"Could we look over the ground a bit?" Land asked. "I see trees and in those trees I imagine there are animals. I wouldn't mind sinking my teeth into a little good meat."

Captain Nemo readily agreed to the idea. The following morning, we left in the *Nautilus* dinghy loaded with guns and axes. No member of the crew came with us, and Land was in charge of sailing the boat.

Land could barely contain his joy and acted like a convict who had broken out of jail. He kept repeating, "We're going to eat meat."

"Stop it," Conseil commanded. "You're making my mouth water."

"We don't even know if there's game in these forests," I said.

"Whatever we find," Land said, "I'm eating it."

When we reached the island, I joined in the excitement at being on dry land again. We strode across the beach and entered the wooded area immediately. Land found a coconut tree and knocked several down. We drank the milk and ate the fruit with delight.

"We should take some of these back to the *Nautilus*," Land said and so we gathered a supply. Then we continued our exploration.

We were able to add breadfruit to our supplies. Land insisted on cooking some immediately and set about building a fire. Then, he cut the breadfruit into thick slices and put them on the hot coals of the fire.

After several minutes, the outside of each slice was completely toasted while the inside had turned to a kind of white paste that tasted a bit like artichoke.

We pressed on and gathered bananas, mangoes, and pineapple. We carried our new-found treasures back to the ship.

We returned the next day. Soon, Land had shot a number of birds. We ate pigeon and dove for lunch. Then Conseil was able to capture a bird of paradise without firing a single shot. I wished desperately that I could carry the beautiful bird back to Paris alive and present it to the Botanical Gardens!

It was shortly after this that Land fulfilled his hopes for our adventure. He shot and cleaned a wild boar. We would have chops for our evening meal.

As we ate this meal on the beach, Land suggested we hide on the island and never return to the *Nautilus*. Just as he spoke, a stone landed at our feet.

We leaped up. Twenty or so natives armed with bows and slings walked slowly toward us.

Land tucked the boar meat under one arm and gathered the rest of our supplies as fast as he could. We pushed the dinghy into the water.

The men on the beach ran into the water after us, shouting and waving their arms. Land and Conseil rowed hard and we reached the *Nautilus* quickly.

I rushed to warn Captain Nemo about the hostile natives. I found him seated at the keyboard of the huge organ in the lounge.

"Calm down, Professor," he said. "There is nothing to worry about."

"But there are a lot of them," I said. By the time we'd reached the *Nautilus*, the beach had filled with at least a hundred people.

"If every man and woman of New Guinea were gathered on the beach," he said, "the *Nautilus* would still have no reason to fear."

Then the captain turned back to the keys of the organ, and I was left to worry alone.

# CHAPTER 10

# The Indian Ocean

During the entire period of low tide, natives continued to gather until their numbers reached 500 or 600. They were handsome people with broad foreheads and athletic builds. They dyed their naturally dark hair red and wore bone earrings.

Land was quite disappointed that we would be doing no more hunting on the island. I spent the time dredging the clear water for unique seashells. Conseil readily agreed to help.

"If Monsieur doesn't mind my saying so," Conseil began as he glanced toward the crowded shore. "They don't seem to have bad intentions."

"Even so, I am happy to have them there and us here," I said as I found the loveliest hammer shell in the dredge. Conseil and I were admiring it when a stone thrown by a native shattered the shell in Conseil's hand.

I gasped. There were twenty or so canoes heading for the *Nautilus*. The boats were made from hollowed-out tree trunks with bamboo floats on the sides. Apparently they had overcome their nervousness around the *Nautilus*.

Suddenly, a cloud of arrows landed on the ship and we wisely went below. Nemo was no more concerned that he had been before. He simply called for the hatches to be closed.

"But what will we do for fresh air?" I asked.

"We will open the hatches tomorrow and let the air in," he said.

"And the natives?" I argued.

Nemo only smiled, and I was left to worry until the following morning. The tide was on the rise, and I could already feel the *Nautilus* shifting on the reef. Nemo called for the hatches to be opened.

The hatch lids opened outward. Twenty horrible faces appeared in the opening, but the first to put a hand on the railing of the companionway was thrown back by some invisible force. He ran off shouting and jumping about wildly. Others tried to enter and suffered the same fate.

Land rushed for the companionway, perhaps thinking to defend us against attack. But as soon as he grabbed the railing, he too was thrown back.

"I've been struck by lightning," he cried.

Then I understood. Nemo had used electricity to drive away the attackers. The natives returned to their boats and their islands. The *Nautilus* drifted free of the reef. We were back on our voyage again.

We continued on our journey but never again passed quite so close to inhabited land. We headed toward the Indian Ocean so that Captain Nemo could conduct experiments in water temperatures at different depths.

During this time, Captain Nemo spotted something from the platform that seemed to cause him great alarm. I rushed to get my own telescope, but he struck it from my hand and asked that I follow his men below.

Land, Conseil, and I were once more locked into the room where we had begun our voyage. A meal was laid out for us. Conseil and Land ate heartily but I barely picked at the food.

When Conseil and Land finished their meal, they immediately settled down on the floor

and fell asleep. I was amazed they could rest when so much was unknown. Then I felt a strange sleepiness as well. The food! I realized we had been drugged by the food.

I fought to keep my eyes open and my mind clear, but soon I joined my friends on the floor, deeply asleep.

I awoke to find myself in my own cabin, laying in my bed. I headed up to the platform. Conseil and Land were already there. We looked across the empty ocean but saw no sign of whatever had caused Nemo to send us below.

Soon after, Nemo sought me out and asked, "Have you studied medicine? Are you a doctor?"

"Yes," I said. "I practiced for several years before starting my work at the museum in Paris."

He nodded solemnly. "Would you mind treating one of my men?"

I agreed and Nemo led me to the crew quarters. The patient lay in his bunk with his head wrapped in bloodstained bandages. His breathing was slow and his arms felt cold.

When I removed the bandages, I saw there was nothing I could do. His skull had been smashed. I put fresh bandages over the wound and sadly told Nemo that the man would be dead soon.

"Nothing can save him?"

"Nothing."

Tears appeared in the captain's eyes. "One of the levers broke in the engine room and struck him on the head," he said sadly, his eyes never leaving the dying man's face.

I left and saw no more of Nemo that day, though I thought I heard a kind of sad singing. The next morning, the captain asked me if my friends and I would like to make another underwater walk.

When we agreed, he sent us to change into our diving suits. We stepped out onto the ocean floor along with Nemo and a dozen crew members who carried a long bundle.

We walked through a beautiful forest of coral before the captain called us to a halt. We had reached a clearing in this coral forest.

I noticed that the ocean floor was marked by regularly shaped mounds. In the center stood a crude cross from blood red coral.

The clearing was a graveyard. Nemo's men carried the body of the man who had died from his terrible head wound. The men dug a grave slowly then lowered the body into it. My two companions and I stood apart but bowed our heads in respect.

Finally the men covered the grave, leaving a fresh mound and we started back for the *Nautilus* immediately. After I changed, I went up to the platform to think about what I had seen. Nemo soon joined me.

"He rests in our peaceful cemetery beyond the reach of sharks and men," Nemo said quietly, then buried his face in his hands.

# A Pearl of Ten Millions

I was beginning to suspect that Captain Nemo had not created the *Nautilus* merely to flee from humanity but to accomplish some kind of revenge. Nemo had locked us up and drugged us while something happened that brought about the death of one of his crew.

These things made me wonder if the *Nautilus* might have attacked another ship. Still, I knew better than to ask.

Never had I felt such conflict. I wanted to see all the wonders the *Nautilus* offered, but I did not want to be a part of attacks on other ships.

We were traveling due west now, through the Indian Ocean. Conseil and I kept busy with our studies, but Land grew more and more restless and short-tempered. Finally, he approached me, pressing me to plan our escape. I put him off, but I knew that would not last.

We passed a school of Argonauts, a type of mollusk sometimes called the Nautilus. These creatures have eight tentacles like a tiny squid but live inside a spiral shell. They move by squirting water though a tube, jetting them through the water.

"The Argonaut never leaves its shell," I said to Conseil.

"Just like Captain Nemo," he wisely answered. "No wonder he calls his ship the *Nautilus*."

It was soon after this that Captain Nemo issued another invitation. "Ceylon is famous for its pearl fisheries," he said. "Would you like to visit one?"

I said I would. He told me we would not likely see any fishermen, as the season had not yet begun.

"The actual fishing is done by men who dive while holding a rock between their feet to pull them down. They cannot stay under for long, and the frequent deep diving is unhealthy. It's not unusual for them to die of stroke."

"What a sad way to earn a living," I murmured. "I hope they make a good wage."

"About a dollar a week," he said, his eyes flashing. "Their employers get rich from the pearls."

Then as Nemo left the lounge, he added that the pearl waters were full of sharks, but that I would get used to them. I stared after him in horror. I could not imagine diving with sharks!

I considered backing out of the adventure, but Conseil and Land seemed eager. I told them how pearls are formed by oysters covering a small irritating bit of grit with layers and layers of mother of pearl. But my explanations were marred by my nervousness.

"Some oysters are veritable jewel boxes. I even read of one oyster that contained 150 sharks."

"Sharks?" Land echoed.

"Oh, I meant pearls." I continued my recitation but sharks crept in over and over. Finally, I admitted that we would be exploring waters where sharks lived in great numbers. I was certain Land and Conseil would refuse to come and then I could back out as well, but that was not the case.

"I'm a professional harpooner," Land said grinning. "It's my job to laugh at sharks."

"If Monsieur is willing to face sharks," Conseil added, "his faithful servant is willing, too."

The *Nautilus* couldn't travel in the shallow waters close to shore, so we took the dinghy. We would put on our suits once we reached the pearl beds.

When the dinghy dropped anchor in the shallow water, Nemo said, "In a month, this narrow bay will be filled with fishermen and their boats."

I did not answer. I peered into the water but couldn't spot any sharks. Finally I asked, "What about our guns?"

"Guns? Here's a sturdy knife. Put it in your belt and we'll be off."

Conseil and Nemo carried knives as well. Land carried a harpoon he'd brought from the *Nautilus,* and that made me feel slightly better.

The sailors helped us overboard and we walked slowly into the deeper water. Nemo pointed to an enormous mass of pearl oysters. Land began filling a sack with oysters, but the captain signaled for us to follow him. He led us to a vast cave in a pile of seaweed-covered rock.

Nemo entered and we followed. The inside was dim but clear enough as our eyes adjusted. We walked down a rather steep slope to the bottom of a circular pit. There rested an oyster of amazing size. It was seven feet wide and must have weighed over 600 pounds.

The creature's two valves were partly open and the captain used his dagger to hold the edges open as he thrust his hand inside. He lifted up the fringed membrane inside to show a huge pearl nestled in the leaf-like folds.

I realized the captain was allowing this pearl to "ripen" and grow bigger with each passing year. Already it must be worth at least 2 million dollars. Who knew what size it might reach someday?

After visiting the giant oyster, we wandered around the pearl beds. Suddenly, we spotted a man diving. Clearly this lone diver had come

early to the beds, driven maybe by need. The diver didn't see us.

Suddenly a shark shot out of the shadows, racing toward the diver. The diver struggled to swim to his boat but was struck by the shark's tail and knocked deeper into the water.

Captain Nemo moved swiftly between shark and diver. He grabbed the shark's fin and buried his dagger in the shark's belly. The creature thrashed as Nemo struck again and again. Finally, the creature twisted and threw the captain to the sea floor.

The bleeding animal turned on the captain, rushing at him with gaping jaws. Land hurled his harpoon, striking a fatal blow to the shark. Then Nemo and Land spotted the diver sinking toward the sea floor, clearly unconscious.

They brought the man to the surface and he regained consciousness, coughing and gagging. Nemo handed the man a bag of pearls, surely worth more than the man would see in a lifetime.

At a sign from the captain, we returned to the oyster bed and then to the dinghy. As our helmets were removed, Captain Nemo said, "Thank you, Master Land."

"I owed you that," Land said.

A vague smile played on the captain's lips and that was all. As the dinghy sped back to the *Nautilus*, we came across a mass of churning water kicked up by dozens of sharks feeding on the one Land had killed.

When we were once again aboard the *Nautilus*, I asked Nemo about his gift to the diver.

"The Indian people live in a land of the oppressed," he said. "In this, we are brothers."

# The Arabian Tunnel

From the Indian Ocean, we sailed toward the Gulf of Oman and then into the Persian Gulf and on to the Red Sea. It seemed we were sailing toward a dead end.

"We will arrive in the Mediterranean the day after tomorrow," Nemo told me.

I gaped in surprise. Backtracking and then sailing around the Cape of Good Hope would take longer than that, even at the speeds the *Nautilus* could travel.

"How can that be?" I asked.

"Through an underground passage, which I call the Arabian Tunnel," he said. "It starts beneath Suez and ends in the Gulf of Pelusium."

"An underwater tunnel connecting two seas," Land said. "Who ever heard of such a thing?"

Conseil laughed. "Who ever heard of the *Nautilus*?"

When we neared Suez, we dove to a depth of thirty or thirty-five feet. Nemo invited me to watch in the helmsman's compartment. It was a small cabin with four portholes that permitted the helmsman to see in all directions.

"Now," Nemo said, "let's find the tunnel."

I looked out in silence at the high wall of solid rock that formed the base of the sandy mountains of the coast. We followed the wall for an hour before I heard a deep rumbling. It was the sound of the water rushing down a sloping tunnel from the Red Sea to the Mediterranean.

The *Nautilus* shot into the tunnel. My heart raced at our speed until we shot out into the Mediterranean Sea. We had rocketed through the tunnel in less than twenty minutes.

At dawn, we surfaced and Land pointed at the coast in the distance. He told me quietly that when the right opportunity showed itself, he would escape. He asked if he could count on me to come along.

"Conseil will do what you do," Land said. "I need only know what you will do."

"I think this opportunity you hope for will not come up," I said quietly. "But if it does, I am with you."

Later I stood peering out the lounge's windows. I spotted a man swimming in the sea with a small leather bag attached to his belt. The man drew nearer until he pressed his face against the glass.

Captain Nemo motioned to him. The diver waved and then headed to the surface. He did not reappear.

"That's Nicholas from Cape Matapan. He is a marvelous diver and lives more in water than on land."

"And you know him," I said, shocked.

"Why shouldn't I, Monsieur Aronnax?" he asked.

The next day, I noticed the *Nautilus* was beginning to heat up. Since the temperature under the sea tends to be cool, even in the Tropics, I wondered at the heat. Was there something wrong with the ship? Was the *Nautilus* on fire?

"We're cruising through a current of boiling water," Captain Nemo told me when I tracked him down.

"How is that possible?"

He opened the panels and I could see the ocean around us was completely white. The glass was too hot to touch.

"I wanted to show you an underwater volcano," the captain said. "Look, you can see it going on right now beneath the surface."

Iron salts in the water were turning it from white to red. Scarlet flames shone brighter than the electric lights. The heat became unbearable and I could smell sulfur. Nemo gave the order and the *Nautilus* veered off, drawing away from the dangerous furnace.

After that, we traveled swiftly and Land grumbled at never having an opportunity to try an escape. Within forty-eight hours, we had slipped through the Strait of Gibraltar and entered the Atlantic Ocean.

Finally, we entered Vigo Bay where the men of the *Nautilus* mined for gold and silver in the simplest possible way. They plucked it from a sunken Spanish galleon. I asked Nemo what he did with all the wealth he stockpiled.

"Do you think, Monsieur, that this wealth is lost when I gather it? Do you think I don't know that there is suffering and oppression on Earth, poor people to be comforted, and victims to be avenged?"

I began to suspect Nemo was doing far more than exploring the ocean. He was funding the oppressed to overthrow their oppressors. Nemo might have run away from society, but it seemed he may not have entirely run away from war.

By the middle of February, the *Nautilus* changed to a heading of south by southwest.

Captain Nemo invited me on another underwater excursion.

"So far you've only seen the ocean depths when the sun is out," he said. "How would you like to see them at night?"

"Very much."

"Splendid. Let's go put on our diving suits."

When I got to the dressing room, I saw that neither my friends nor any crew members were to go with us. In a few minutes we had put on our suits, but we had no light. I asked about that and Nemo said we would not need one.

Several minutes later we set foot on the floor of the Atlantic at a depth of about 1,000 feet. The water was completely dark, but Nemo pointed toward a reddish glow about two miles away. Although I had no idea how a fire was burning in the water, it lit our way.

The flat ground rose as we walked. We took large strides but progress was slow, as our feet often sank in the soft ocean floor. I heard a kind of crackling and soon realized it was rain pounding down on the surface of the ocean. For a moment I worried about getting wet, and the foolishness of that thought made me laugh.

The ground grew steeper and more rocky. When I turned, I could still make out the light from the *Nautilus* growing paler in the distance. I began to realize the rocks were laid out on the ocean floor in a regular pattern.

What was this strange place we were crossing? We walked always facing the reddish glow and I wondered if this was some electrical beacon placed by Captain Nemo. I even thought perhaps we would find people living on the ocean floor in some fantastic dwelling.

Eventually, we reached the foot of a mountain covered by a forest of trees petrified by the sea. I climbed the rocks and fallen tree trunks like a lizard.

As we neared the top of the mountain, I realized it was a volcano. The lava was the red

glow that we followed. Then Nemo pointed downward, and I looked down upon stone buildings in ruins. The style reminded me of an acropolis or the Parthenon. Where was I?

Captain Nemo took me by the arm. He picked up a piece of chalky stone and wrote a word on the black rock: Atlantis!

We stayed there for a whole hour contemplating the ruined city. Sometimes the mountain rumbled. Finally the captain straightened up and motioned for me to follow him.

When we reached the bottom of the mountain, I could see the *Nautilus*'s light shining like a star. We were back on board as the first rays of the sun whitened the surface of the ocean.

# The South Pole

After visiting Atlantis, you would think there would be no greater wonders for us. But within two days I was struck speechless again.

I had made my normal morning climb to the platform. The hatch was open, but instead of the bright daylight I expected, I found myself surrounded by total darkness. Not a single star was shining and I had never seen a night so dark. I didn't know what to think, when suddenly a voice said, "Is that you, Professor?"

"Captain Nemo, where are we?" I answered.

"Underground."

"Underground?" I cried. "But the *Nautilus* is floating."

It was so dark that I could not see Captain Nemo at all. Far above I could make out a faint glimmer filtering through a round hole. Then a strong search light was turned on and for a moment my eyes were completely dazzled.

I blinked a few times and looked around. The *Nautilus* was moored to a bank shaped like a dock. It was floating in a lake within circular walls two miles in diameter.

"We are at the center of an extinct volcano," the captain said. "This is my harbor. It is safe, secret, and sheltered from any wind. It is here my men mine for coal to make the sodium for the batteries that produce our electricity."

"Will I see your companions do this?"

"No, not this time. I'm in a hurry to continue our tour. I will merely take sodium from my reserve stock. We should be here about a day. Perhaps you would like to take a walk around the lake with your friends."

My friends and I spent the day climbing the sides of the volcano as high as we could go. Eventually the walls curved in too sharply to continue. Near the end of our climb, Land found a beehive and collected honey to bring back.

We climbed back down and felt the better for having some time to walk on land again. By the next day, the *Nautilus* had left its port and returned to cruising the Atlantic.

The *Nautilus* continued to head south. We stayed well away from land, and I know Land was frustrated by the lack of opportunities for escape. I began to worry about him, for I noticed that his ill will toward Captain Nemo was increasing.

By mid-March, I fully expected that we would go around Cape Horn and return to the South Pacific, but we did nothing of the sort. The *Nautilus* merely continued in the direction of the Antarctic.

Could the captain be trying to reach the South Pole? This was a feat no man had managed. Soon twenty-foot chunks of floating ice began to appear in the water.

Toward the southern horizon there was a shining white streak in the sky. English whalers call it "ice blink." Such streaks signal the presence of a sizable ice bank. We began to spot real icebergs. We saw petrels and puffins nesting on the ice.

Captain Nemo truly showed his skills as we moved through the ice. Often the horizon seemed completely blocked, but after a careful search, Nemo would slip through a narrow opening. When the ice blocked us completely, Nemo sent the *Nautilus* hurling against it, splitting the ice like a wedge.

The temperature plummeted below freezing. We wore seal and polar bear furs on the platform. The inside of the *Nautilus* stayed warm with electric heat.

Finally on March 18, the *Nautilus* reached a wall of ice that could not be broken.

"The Great Ice Barrier!" Land exclaimed.

We had reached a point where no ship could go farther. But the *Nautilus* was not like any other ship. Nemo insisted we were going to the pole.

"Will you put wings on the *Nautilus* and fly over this?" I asked, pointing at the wall of ice.

"No, not over it," Captain Nemo said calmly. "Under it. Though the surface of the sea is frozen, the deeper water is free. The only difficulty will be if we have to stay under too many days without renewing our air supply."

That truly was a problem I hoped we would not meet.

The *Nautilus* dove below the ice and rushed ahead. It was now a race to find open water before our air grew foul. Ultimately, it seemed almost too easy, and we stayed only one day longer than usual below water. Captain Nemo did not even need to call upon his reserves.

We could see ice and rocks in the distance ahead and we took the dinghy to land. Captain Nemo climbed out of the small boat, making him the first man to step foot on the land surrounding the South Pole.

Now we had only to take readings to find the exact pole. Unfortunately, the weather was thickly cloudy for days. We went back and forth from the land to the ship, watching for a glimpse of sun to allow Nemo to verify our location.

I did not mind the wait so terribly. I saw thousands of sea birds soaring above us. On the rocks, penguin nests covered the ground. The noisy, waddling birds showed no fear when we passed among them. We also spotted various kinds of seals.

Finally on March 21, our last chance to verify our position arrived. After this, the eternal Antarctic night would settle over the pole. We had to see the sun at exactly noon for an accurate reading.

The weather cleared for just the right instant and Captain Nemo was able to verify our location. We had indeed walked on the South Pole.

# Want of Air

The temperature fell and the water grew thick with ice. The *Nautilus* sank below the surface and headed north as swiftly as we dared.

In the middle of that first night, I was awakened by a violent blow that hurled me from my bed. The *Nautilus* had collided with something and heeled over a sharp angle.

I stumbled into the lounge and found Conseil and Land looking equally distressed. The pressure gauge showed we were at a depth of 1,180 feet. We had struck something well below the surface.

When the captain entered, I asked him flatly, "Has the *Nautilus* run aground?"

"Yes. An enormous block of ice has turned over and struck the *Nautilus*."

"Can the *Nautilus* rise?"

Captain Nemo nodded. "It can and it is. Unfortunately, the ice is rising with us."

I could see the problem immediately. We would eventually collide with the underside of the Great Ice Barrier. If the ice below us continued to rise, we would be trapped and perhaps crushed between the two slabs of ice.

We all watched the pressure gauge in silence as the *Nautilus* continued to rise. Finally, we seemed to outrun the ice under us. The *Nautilus* slowly righted itself. The panels in the wall opened and we could see our position more clearly.

We were suspended in the water with ice walls thirty feet away on each side. We were walled in above and below as well. The *Nautilus* rushed forward for a time, then changed direction and ran backward.

Eventually, a second collision took place behind us. The *Nautilus* was trapped. We had been underwater for 36 hours. We had enough

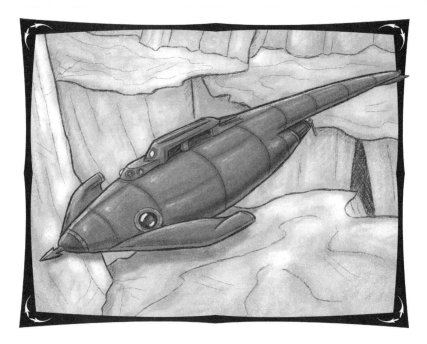

air in reserve for 48 more hours. After that, everyone aboard the *Nautilus* would die.

"Do you have a plan?" I asked the captain.

"My men will put on their diving suits and start to work on breaking up the ice where it is thinnest. If we can make a small hole, the *Nautilus* can then make a big one."

Conseil, Land, and I all volunteered to help. The water was bitterly cold, but we soon became warm as we swung the pickax. Each time we left the ship for a shift of ice breaking and returned, we noticed how much worse the air in the ship had become.

The ice breaking was slow work and it soon became clear it would not rescue us. We needed another idea. Captain Nemo began shooting hot water from the huge tank in a kitchen out into the cold, raising the temperature and thinning the ice further. We continued with the work of ice breaking.

The hours we spent aboard were horrible. I felt as if I were choking to death constantly. My companions had the same symptoms, and some members of the crew were close to death.

Finally Nemo decided it was time to send the *Nautilus* crashing against the ice we had thinned. No more air was available for working or resting. He slammed the *Nautilus* against the thinned ice and it broke! We were free of our ice prison!

Still, we had to reach the edge of the Great Ice Barrier quickly. The reserves were gone. There wasn't enough air to keep us alive.

Finally I passed out, only to find myself revived again. My dear friends had carried one of the diving tanks to my cabin and given me the last few breaths of air it contained.

I sat up and staggered to the lounge. The gauges showed the *Nautilus* moving at a staggering forty knots. The ship trembled from the effort. Then, it slammed into the ice field from below like a battering ram, knocking me to the floor again.

The ship rushed through the layer of ice. The hatch was opened and pure air flooded into the *Nautilus*. Land and Conseil half carried me to the platform and we gasped in the purest of air.

The *Nautilus* stayed above the surface now and traveled fast. We reached the tip of the American continent by March 31. The days that followed were especially pleasant, coming on the heels of so close a brush with death. We reached the equator by April 10, and still we rushed north.

# CHAPTER
## 15

# Giant Squid

On April 20, we reached the Bahamas. The islands spread out like paving stones on the water's surface. Deep below we saw high underwater cliffs full of dark holes so deep our searchlights could not penetrate them.

"Those are the kinds of caves giant squid live in," I said.

Conseil leaned closer to the viewing window. "I'd like to come face-to-face with one of the giant squid that can drag ships to the bottom."

"You'll never get me to believe such animals exist," said Land.

"Certainly octopus and squid can grow to great size," I said. "The *Alecton* nearly captured one not far from here. Commander Bourguer managed to bring back a piece of it."

"Was it about twenty feet long?" Conseil asked. He was standing at the window and once more examining the rugged cliffs.

"Precisely," I said.

"Was its head crowned with eight tentacles that thrashed about on the water like a nest of snakes?" Conseil went on. "And did it have huge popping eyes? Was its mouth like a parrot's beak, but enormous?"

"That's right."

"Well then," Conseil replied calmly, "this is either Bouguer's squid or one of its cousins."

Land and I rushed to the window. Before our eyes a terrible monster swam toward the *Nautilus*. It had huge, sea-green eyes. Its eight twisting arms were twice as long as its body.

I could make out suckers lining the inside of its tentacles, some of which fastened on the glass window of the lounge. The monster's horny beak opened and closed against the glass.

Seven other squid appeared outside the starboard window. They swam around the

*Nautilus*. I could hear the noise of their beaks grinding on the steel hull. Suddenly the *Nautilus* stopped. A sharp blow sent a quiver through the ship.

Captain Nemo entered the lounge with his first mate. He peered through the glass panel at the squid, then gave a command to the first mate, who left quickly.

"Have we struck ground?" I asked.

"The propeller has been stopped," he replied. "I think one of these squid is caught in the propeller and now we can't move. To safely clear the propeller, we must surface the ship and fight the squid."

Land said, "If you'll permit me, I'll help you."

"I will accept any help."

We followed Captain Nemo to the central companionway. There, ten or twelve men armed with axes were ready for the attack. Conseil and I each took an ax, and Land took a harpoon.

One of the sailors opened the hatch. The long arm of a squid slid into the opening. With one blow of his ax, Nemo cut the tentacle and it flopped to the floor of the companionway.

Two other arms slashed down through the opening and grabbed a sailor. It jerked him through the hatch in an instant. Nemo shouted and rushed onto the platform. We followed.

The sailor was clutched by the tentacles and waved around in the air. Nemo hurled himself at the squid and cut off another arm. All of us began flailing away at the monsters that were climbing up the sides of the *Nautilus*.

For a moment I thought the poor man would be saved. Seven of the creature's arms were hacked off, only the one holding the man remained. Just as Nemo rushed at it, the creature flung itself into the sea and disappeared with the crewman.

We continued to hack at the remaining creatures. Suddenly Land was knocked to the floor. The blow slid him almost to the edge, where the beak of the monster snapped at him.

The poor man was about to be cut in two, but Captain Nemo buried his ax between the two enormous jaws. Land was saved.

"I owed you this," said Captain Nemo.

The struggle lasted fifteen minutes before the monsters finally slid into the sea and bothered us no more.

The captain retired to his cabin and I didn't see him again for some time. The *Nautilus* no longer stayed on a fixed course. It floated like a corpse at the mercy of the waves for ten days.

# CHAPTER 16

# A Hecatomb

On May 1, the *Nautilus* once again started on a definite northern course. We entered the greatest ocean current, the Gulf Stream.

We followed the Gulf Stream up to Cape Hatteras, not far from the coast of North Carolina. We saw neither captain nor crew. It seemed the perfect time to plan an escape. But then a violent storm roared in.

As the storm raged, the captain climbed to the platform and tied himself to the railing against the huge waves breaking over the ship.

I followed him and also tied myself so that I might see what had brought him out to face such danger. The violence of the storm increased as night came on.

By ten o'clock, I felt crushed and at the end of my strength. I crawled on my stomach to the hatch, opened it, and went back down into the lounge. Captain Nemo came back in about midnight. Soon after, the *Nautilus* sank below the surface and we continued north to Newfoundland.

I felt some concern that Nemo might decide to conquer the North Pole as he had the South, but the *Nautilus* turned east to open water. By May 28, we were no more than 100 miles from Ireland. We turned south then, toward continental waters and proceeded slowly.

During the day of May 31, the *Nautilus* went around in a circular course. Captain Nemo seemed more somber than ever. He stood on the platform to sight our position and it was obvious we were trying to find some exact spot on the ocean. The sea was calm, the sky clear.

Eight miles to the east, a large steamship was outlined against the horizon. I could not tell its nationality. Captain Nemo seemed to pay it no attention at all.

Finally Nemo called out, "It's here!" He motioned for me to follow them down off the platform. I gave one last look at the steamship. I believed it was bearing down on us, but I could not say for sure.

The *Nautilus* dropped to a depth of almost 3,000 feet. The lounge's panels opened and I could see the ocean brilliantly. To starboard, a large object stuck up from the ocean floor. It was a large ship that had sunk bow first.

Captain Nemo walked up behind me. "Today, Monsieur, is the first of June, 1868. Seventy-four years ago on this exact spot, after a heroic struggle, the crew of that ship preferred to go down rather than surrender. As it disappeared beneath the surface, 356 sailors shouted, 'Long live the Republic!'"

"The *Revenge*!" I cried.

"That's right. The *Revenge*. What a lovely name!" the captain murmured.

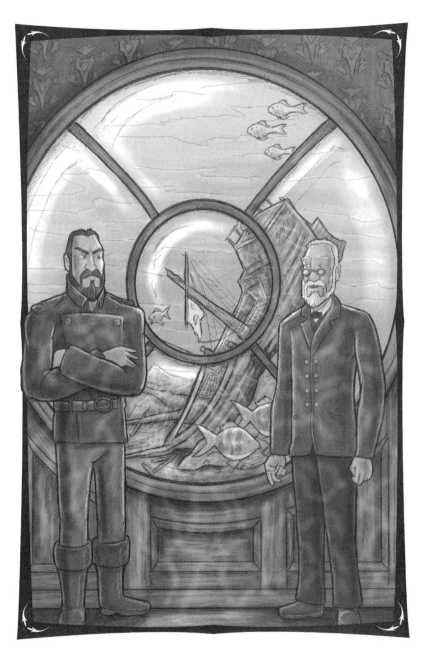

After that, the *Nautilus* rose back to the surface. Suddenly, I heard a dull explosion. "What's that?" I asked.

Nemo did not answer. I left him alone and hurried up to the platform. My friends were there.

"They're firing on us," Land said. "That's a warship but I can't tell what country it is from. I do know that if the ship comes within a mile of us, I'm going to jump into the water."

"But they're firing on us," I cried. "So clearly they do not believe we are shipwrecked men clinging to our overturned craft."

"I believe they know exactly what we are," Land said.

That's when it became clear. Undoubtedly people now knew what the so-called monster really was. Throughout the world's oceans, ships probably pursued this terrible weapon. Land took out his handkerchief to wave in the air, but it was snatched from his hand.

"You fool," Captain Nemo shouted. "I should nail you to the prow before I ram that ship." He ordered us to go below. "They have attacked us, and the counterattack will be terrible."

The *Nautilus* dropped below the surface and increased speed considerably. The entire hull trembled. I felt a light blow and heard chafing and scraping sounds. The *Nautilus* went right through the hull of the ship like a needle through cloth.

Captain Nemo joined me in the lounge where the windows opened to show the ship sinking. At first the ship sank slowly, but then there was an explosion of the compressed air inside the hull. It sank faster after that.

I saw the crow's nest filled with sailors and the cross trees bending under the weight of the men hanging to them. The ship disappeared past us.

After that, the *Nautilus* fled north at twenty-five knots and we soon entered the English Channel.

# CHAPTER 17

# The Last Words of Captain Nemo

I no longer saw anything of Captain Nemo or his first mate. Not a single member of his crew appeared on the platform. I felt sick to be part of the destruction of the steamship and its crew. The voyage no longer held any joy for me.

One morning, I was awakened by someone shaking me. I opened my eyes to see Land. He whispered, "This is our chance."

I sat up. "When?"

"Tonight. We will meet at the dinghy at ten o'clock. I've seen land about twenty miles to the east."

"What country is it?"

"I don't know, but whatever country it is, we're going to take refuge there."

"Good, Ned. We'll go tonight, even if the sea swallows us up."

"If we're caught," Land said grimly, "I'm going to defend myself, even if I die doing it."

"We'll die together, my friend."

After that, the day passed slowly. I took one last look at the wonders of nature and the masterpieces of art on the ship. I dined at six, but I was not hungry. Then I went to my room and dressed in thick sea clothes.

I got my notes together and tucked them carefully inside my jacket. Then with just a half an hour to go, I heard the faint music of the organ. The captain was in the lounge, through which I had to pass in order to escape. But I could not hesitate, even with the captain in my way.

I opened my door carefully and crept forward along the gangways of the *Nautilus*. I opened the door to the lounge quietly. Nemo never turned away from his organ. I crept across the carpet and was about to open the next door when a sigh from Nemo froze me. I heard him murmur, "Dear God, enough! Enough!"

I slipped through the door and hurried down the companionway until I reached the dinghy. My two companions were already inside. Land had brought along a wrench. He closed and bolted the hatch then began unfastening the bolts that held us to the *Nautilus*.

Suddenly we heard the sound of rushing feet and voices. We froze, but I soon realized we were not causing the excitement among the crew.

"The maelstrom!" they cried.

The maelstrom! Were we in the dangerous waters off the coast of Norway? There, the waters between the Lofoten and Faeroe islands rush out with the tide with great force. They form a whirlpool that no ship has ever escaped. The *Nautilus* was in this whirlpool.

The ship spun faster and faster in smaller and smaller circles. The whirling made me dizzy and sick to my stomach.

"We have to hold on," said Land. "Screw the bolts back down! Our only chance is to stay attached to the *Nautilus*!"

He had hardly finished the sentence when we heard a loud cracking sound. The bolts had given way. The dinghy was torn from its socket and thrown out into the middle of the sea, like a stone hurled from a sling. My head hit an iron rib and I lost consciousness.

Thus ended our voyage beneath the seas. I do not know how the dinghy escaped the whirlpool. I do not know why we are alive. I awoke lying in a fisherman's cottage on one of the Lofoten islands. My two friends were sitting next to me, and I greeted them with great emotion.

We are now waiting for the steamboat that sails twice a month from North Cape. With that we will begin our journey home. Will people believe all that we've seen and done? I do not know. It makes little difference. No one can deny me the right to speak of it.

In less than ten months, I have traveled 20,000 leagues, much of it under the sea.

But what happened to the *Nautilus*? Did it escape as we escaped? Will I ever know its destiny? I hope so.

I hope Captain Nemo still inhabits the ocean. And I hope for peace for his savage heart. He has shown me much, and I will never forget.